THE
SPECKLEDY HEN

BASED ON THE STORIES BY

Alison Uttley and *Margaret Tempest*

An imprint of HarperCollins*Publishers*

The Speckledy Hen was first
published in 1945 by William Collins Sons & Co
This edition was first published in Great Britain by HarperCollins*Publishers* Ltd in 2001

1 3 5 7 9 10 8 6 4 2
ISBN: 0-00-710259-3

Text for this edition by Susan Dickinson based on the
television adaptation by Helen Cresswell
Text © The Alison Uttley Literary Property Trust 2001
Illustrations in this work derived from the television series © HTV LTD 2000
based on the original illustrations by Margaret Tempest.
Production of the television series by United Productions in association with Cosgrove Hall.

A CIP catalogue record for this title is available from the British Library.

The HarperCollins website address is: www.**fire**and**water**.com

Printed and bound in Hong Kong

I T WAS SPRING. The primroses and cowslips were out in the fields. The violets were blue in the hedgerows where the birds were building their nests. And the Speckledy Hen slipped away from the noisy farmyard with all its hustle and bustle, and set off to look for a little house of her own.

She looked all around, but every house seemed to be occupied by some small creature, until she came to a large oak tree by the stream.

"Very comfortable and just the right size for a nursery," she clucked. Back she went to the farmyard to collect her things.

"And where are you going, dear Speckledy Hen?" asked the Cock.

"That's a secret," clucked the Speckledy Hen.

On her way back to the old oak tree she met Hare.

"Hullo!" he cried. "Where are you going looking so handsome and fat?"

"Off to make a secret," she replied.

"Mind you don't meet the Fox!" warned Hare.

"Hello, Fuzzypeg," she said when she bumped into the little fellow. "Have you been good today and done your lessons well?"

"Yes. I can read now, even long words like barley sugar," he said proudly.

Speckledy Hen went on her way to settle herself in her new home in the oak tree.

She put all her things away: she put the little loaves and her frying pan on the shelf, and she put her kettle and teapot on the stove in the corner.

She even found a curtain made of bats' wings to hang across the door. Then she made a soft nest of moss and grass, laid her first egg and settled herself on it to keep it warm.

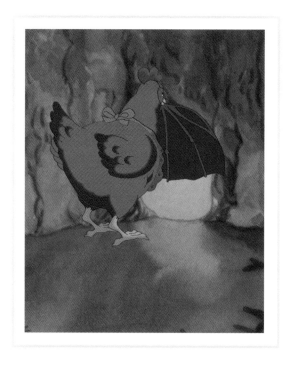

Every day she laid another, until in the nest were ten beautiful eggs. Each morning she slipped out of her house to the stream for a sip of water.

Then she hurried back to keep her eggs warm. She never went back to the farmyard, for then her eggs would have chilled.

The Cock was worried. "Has anyone seen the Speckledy Hen?" he asked. "She went for a walk and never came back." But no one knew where she was.

Hedgehog called at little Grey Rabbit's with the milk and Grey Rabbit ran to the door.

"An extra jugful, please. I'm going to make a cake. Hare is going to the Speckledy Hen for an egg."

"Haven't you heard the news?" exclaimed Hedgehog. "She's gone!"

"Gone?" gasped Squirrel.

"Surely not!" said little Grey Rabbit.

"Nobody hasn't seen so much as a feather of her for more nor a week," said Hedgehog.

"I met her last week going for a walk," said Hare.

"Well, she never came back. And what's more, that there Fox is about," continued Hedgehog.

"Oh darling Speckledy Hen!" cried little Grey Rabbit, and Squirrel burst into tears.

"Now don't take on, Miss Squirrel – here, wipe your bonny eyes on my handkerchief," said Old Hedgehog.

"I don't think the Fox has caught Speckledy Hen," announced little Grey Rabbit. "She's far too clever for him."

"If only I'd taught her to play noughts and crosses!" said Hare. "Then she could escape as I did!"

"Ah, what it must be to have brains," said Hedgehog.

All this time the Speckledy Hen had been sitting on her eggs in her warm little house. She chuckled as she thought of the day when she would lead home a fine brood of chicks.

Meanwhile, the Fox was walking through the wet grass, sniffing. He sniffed and he sniffed, until he came to the little doorway with the bats' wing curtain. He sat down beside the tree and waited till morning.

The Speckledy Hen was asleep on her eggs. In the morning she woke up, drew back the curtain and peeped out. It was a beautiful day.

"Good morning, Missus," said the Fox.

"Shoo! Go away you bad fox!" she scolded. "Buk! Buk! Shoo! Shoo! Buk! Buk!"

"Won't you invite me in?" said the Fox with a smile.

"Shoo! Shoo!" she said again.

"Goodbye then. I must leave you if we can't be friends."
The Fox turned away, but he hid behind the tree.

The Speckledy Hen put on her bonnet and crept to the door. She put out her head and – Snap! Her best bonnet was caught in the Fox's jaws.

"Oh, deary me!" she wailed. "My sweet little bonnet! But it might have been my silly little head! And what would my babies have done without me?"

There was a cheeping and a pecking among the eggs and one by one the little chicks came out of their shells. The Speckledy Hen gathered them under her wings and sang softly to them.

As Fuzzypeg was walking home from school he saw the little bonnet hanging from a furze bush. And close by was the Fox, keeping guard.

Fuzzypeg turned and ran. "Father! Father!" he called when he was nearly home.

"There's a little bonnet hanging on a furze bush! It looks like the Speckledy Hen's."

"Where was it, son?" asked Old Hedgehog.

"Near the stream in the Green Pasture," said Fuzzypeg.

"And – there was a Fox hiding near!"

"That Speckledy Hen has thrown her bonnet at him," said Hedgehog. "She's always been a daring female. But I don't believe he's caught her yet."

"I'll go and tell Grey Rabbit. She'll know what to do!" cried Fuzzypeg.

So off Fuzzypeg ran, through the wood to tell little Grey Rabbit, Hare and Squirrel the news.

"We must do something! Oh, poor Speckledy Hen!" said Grey Rabbit.

"I'll go and ask Wise Owl," said Hare.

"Take him a present!" said Grey Rabbit. "Your old musical box!"

Hare ran through the wood to Wise Owl's house and rang the little silver bell.

"What do you want?" hooted Wise Owl crossly. "And where is my present?"

"Here," said Hare, holding up the musical box. "But please, Wise Owl, how shall we get rid of the Fox? He's after the Speckledy Hen."

"I'll help you," said Wise Owl. "Keep your musical box. You'd better get someone to read a nice story to him."

"B-b-but who? *I'm* not a good reader!
I get stuck on the long words... I hardly
know which way up to hold a book."
Wise Owl threw down a thick
little book.
"Here," he said. "Read it."
Hare went home with the book
under his arm, wondering who
would read to the Fox.

"I can't make head nor tail of it," said Old Hedgehog.

"I can't read long words," said little Grey Rabbit.

"My Fuzzypeg can! He's a scholard – a real scholard!" exclaimed Hedgehog.

So Fuzzypeg set off with the book towards the oak tree, where the Fox sat waiting.

When he got near, he called out, "Mr Fox, I go to school now!"

"Oh, indeed?" said the Fox.

"I can sing," said Fuzzypeg. And he began.

"Oh, John, John, the grey goose is gone, and the fox is in the town-o!"

"Well, that's a good song, Fuzzypeg," said the Fox.

"I can read, too. Shall I read you a tale, Mr Fox?"

"It *is* rather dull waiting here," replied the Fox. "Yes, a good story will cheer me up."

So Fuzzypeg opened the book. "It's called *The Fox and the Grapes*," he said.

In the old oak tree the baby chicks were cheeping.

"Mother, when can we go out?" they asked.

"Soon, soon," said the Speckledy Hen.

"A famished fox," said Fuzzypeg, beginning his story.

The Fox licked his lips. "That's me. A famished fox. I'm getting hungrier and hungrier!"

"A famished fox saw some clusters of black grapes..."

"Rich black grapes," murmured the Fox and he smacked his lips together.

"Quickly," whispered the Speckledy Hen to her little chicks. "When I go, you must follow me!"

"Go on, Fuzzypeg. It does me good to hear a true story, especially about a fox..." said the Fox.

"He resorted to all his tricks to get at them," read Fuzzypeg, "but he could not reach them."

Out of the corner of his eye Fuzzypeg could spy the Speckledy Hen scurrying around collecting her chicks.

Then she seized her bonnet from the furze bush and started off towards home.

"Jemimay!" said the Fox. "Can't reach them, eh? Just like me with the Speckledy Hen and her chicks."

"At last he turned away," continued Fuzzypeg, "saying, 'The grapes are sour and not as ripe as I thought!'"

"How did the fox know they were sour if he hadn't tasted them?" asked the Fox.

"I speck he said it to comfort himself," said Fuzzypeg.

"Yes. Thank you for your nice tale, Fuzzypeg," said the Fox, and he went back to the little door in the oak tree.

"Are you all right, Speckledy Hen?" he called. "Would you like to hear the story of the Fox and the Grapes?" All was quiet.

He peeped in. The little room was empty!

"Bother! Bother! How did she escape?" he growled.

The Fox galloped away through the wood, over the river to his den in the far valley.

"I'm quite sure the Speckledy Hen would have been very tough, even if I had caught her," he said to himself, as he settled back into his rocking chair with the book.

In the farmyard everyone was admiring the Speckledy Hen's family.

"Three cheers for little Fuzzypeg!" cried the Cock, when the Speckledy Hen had finished telling them how he had saved her and her chicks.

"And now I'll make my cake," said little Grey Rabbit, "and we'll have a feast for the Speckledy Hen and her family, and for brave little Fuzzypeg!"